This Walker book belongs to:

_____

_____

A giraffe kiss
is gentle and
tall...

A mouse
kiss
is
quick

and

small...

like this!

kiss

A
fish kiss
is fizzy and

bubbly . . .

like
this!

A bee kiss
is fuzzy

and buzzy...

An
elephant
kiss is
long and
toot-tooty...

An owl kiss is

Other books by Mary Murphy:

978-1-4063-3908-6

978-1-4063-4746-3

shiny touch
Quick Duck!
MARY MURPHY

978-1-4063-3907-9

978-1-4063-3774-7

Utterly Lovely One
MARY MURPHY

978-1-4063-4828-6

flip-flap fun
Mouse Is Small
Mary Murphy

978-1-4063-2996-4

Available from all good booksellers
www.walker.co.uk